Swifty's Big Flight

LEE JACKSON

Illustrated by

RYAN ALEXANDER-TANNER

Tiger RM LLC
Portland, OR

For the Cookie Boy and his helpers

For Leila and Vivian and Emmett and Owen

A special thank you to Charity Heller Hogue of The Mighty Pen for her wordsmith wizardry and to Jennifer Omner at ALL Publications for guiding our book through printing paradise. Our illustrations would not be accurate without the advice and support of Steve Engel at the Portland Audubon Society. A big thank you to Steve for graciously balancing ornithology knowledge with artistic whimsy.

Tiger RM LLC
25 NW 23rd Place, Suite 6, Box 190
Portland, OR 97201
www.flyingswift.blogspot.com

ISBN: 978-0-9820274-0-0

Library of Congress Control Number: 2008907007

"Time to go, little one."

Swifty peered through the morning light at his father, who was hanging from the inside of the family hollow. Today, Swifty was eight weeks old and it was time for his first big flight!

Swifty was a Vaux's Swift. He had taken several short flights, but never beyond view of his home.

It was late summer and Vaux's Swifts were already
disappearing from their hollows to fly from the Pacific
Northwest to Central America, where they would spend
the winter.

"Swifty, we're going to spend the next weeks traveling south before it gets too cold here in the mountains," said Father. "Tonight, when darkness comes again, find the biggest hollow on the edge of the forest where the trees touch the city lights. We'll roost there for the night.

And be on the lookout for hawks. A slow Vaux's Swift is a hawk's favorite meal."

Binky was eager to begin. He loosened his velcro-like grip on the tree wall and fluttered to the top of the hollow.

As he exited, he tucked his feet under his feathers
and zipped into the sky.

Whoosh!

Swifty spiraled in the air, upside down and back
again, flapping his tiny wings rapidly next to the
hundreds of Vaux's Swifts in his colony. The sky was a
maze of black birds, tiny crescent moons twisting and
turning all directions in the wind.

Now this was the way to travel!

As he wove through the air, Swifty gulped breakfast.
"One-hundred...one-hundred-one...one-hundred-two..." he
counted to himself as he gobbled juicy bugs.

Swifty especially liked the flying ballooning spiders,
the ones that float on a strand of their web.

Over the trees and towns and towers Swifty soared.

When he got hungry, he swallowed more bugs. When he got thirsty, the little bird scooped water from a pond with his beak. But he never stopped flying.

"Hey, you!" said a frog on a log. "Why don't you stop and take a load off?"

But Swifty kept flying.

It wasn't that he was in a hurry. Nor was he trying
to be rude. His feet simply couldn't grasp branches like
other birds. "Vaux's Swifts never perch," Father had said.
"Your sharp claws are for hanging on a wall like a picture.
Don't worry about falling backwards. Your tail will help
you keep your balance."

Swifty caught up with his sister, Speedy. "How far do you think we've flown?" Swifty shouted as he zoomed by like a jet fighter.

"Mm . . . about 100 miles," said Speedy. "Let's have lunch."

The birds took turns catching insects.

"Look, I can eat three bugs in one mouthful!" said Swifty.

"I can eat three bugs in one mouthful upside down!" said Speedy.

After lunch, Speedy said, "I'm going to take a nap."
Swifty watched his sister close her eyes and float lazily on
a current of thermal air. Speedy could actually fly while
sleeping!

Swifty was too excited to sleep. Flying was great fun and he wanted to beat his sister to the hollow.

As the sun began to set, Swifty looked for the biggest hollow on the edge of the forest where the trees touched the city lights. Many trees loomed in the distance, but none were particularly tall.

The night was eerily quiet and Swifty was alone.

Suddenly, a shadow drifted over the little Vaux's Swift: a hawk was looking right at him!

Swifty knew he had to find shelter. Fast. But before he could find a safe place—

Bam!

The hawk's wings roughly pushed Swifty to the side. Swifty did his best backward flip to get away from the hawk and dove downward, flapping his wings as fast as he could.

Bam!

The hawk tried to snag Swifty with his sharp talons.
Swifty dove and twirled; he rocketed upward and
downward, flew sideways then twirled again, trying to
lose the hawk. It was hard to see where he was going. The
hawk came at Swifty again.

Bam!

This time, Swifty stumbled into a dark hole and began falling, down, down, down.

When Swifty caught his balance, he found himself
inside a chimney. And then he heard the familiar rustle of
Vaux's Swifts . . . many from his own colony. Luckily, the
chimney opening was so tiny that the hawk couldn't fit
inside.

Even better, Swifty had fallen where his family was roosting.

"Swifty!" said Mother, rushing to his side. "We've been so worried. The big hollow on the edge of the forest where the trees touch the city lights is gone. We hoped you'd see Vaux's Swifts using this chimney and know this was a safe place."

"Good job, son," said Father.

But Swifty was already asleep. He was dreaming of his next big flight.

Facts About Vaux's Swifts

- "Vaux's Swifts" is pronounced "vawks," not "voh."

- Vaux's Swifts are four to five inches long. Their crescent-shaped wings beat rapidly (swiftly)! Vaux's Swifts spend much of their time flying—they eat, drink, court, mate, and collect nesting materials in flight. Vaux's Swifts do not perch. You can find them either flying or clinging to a vertical surface. Their nests hang on the insides of trees or chimneys.

- Vaux's Swifts can be found anywhere from southwestern Canada to the western United States and in Mexico, Central America, and Venezuela. Vaux's Swifts court in May and June. Their eggs are laid and hatched by July. In the fall, Vaux's Swifts gather in large groups as they prepare to migrate south.

- Vaux's Swifts descend head first into their roosting tree or chimney at dusk. Vaux's Swifts roost as a group by the hundreds and sometimes thousands. They huddle together, probably to conserve heat.

- Vaux's Swifts fly an estimated 135,000 miles each year—that's three times around the earth— or about 200 miles per day.

Sources: Cornell Lab of Ornithology, Audubon Society of Portland

ABOUT THE AUTHOR/ILLUSTRATOR

Lee Jackson (www.flyingswift.blogspot.com) is a Portland, Ore., freelance writer who has been watching the Vaux's Swifts from the porch of her Northwest home for the past five years. "Swifty's Big Flight" is Lee's first published children's book.

Ryan Alexander-Tanner (www.ohyesverynice.com) spent all of his time in grade school doodling in the margins. Now he draws pictures for a living. He has created comics and illustrations for a few large companies and a lot of little ones. He is also involved in arts education, having lectured on historical and contemporary comics at several Universities, and taught elementary students Comics Illustration through the SUN (Schools Uniting Neighborhoods) program.